Richard Grant White

The American View of the Copyright Question

Richard Grant White

The American View of the Copyright Question

ISBN/EAN: 9783337419455

Printed in Europe, USA, Canada, Australia, Japan

Cover: Foto ©Andreas Hilbeck / pixelio.de

More available books at **www.hansebooks.com**

THE AMERICAN VIEW

OF THE

COPYRIGHT QUESTION.

Reprinted from the "Broadway Magazine," May, 1868.

WITH A

POSTSCRIPT.

BY

RICHARD GRANT WHITE,

SECRETARY OF THE EXECUTIVE COMMITTEE OF THE COPYRIGHT ASSOCIATION.

—◆

LONDON AND NEW YORK:
GEORGE ROUTLEDGE AND SONS.
—
1880.

ADVERTISEMENT.

DURING the last few years there has been from time to time a " movement" among men of letters and publishers to bring about what is called an International Copyright Law, in which I have been invited personally and by letter to take part. As I have neither done so nor given reasons for withholding myself from agreeable associations in an honorable cause, I may, perhaps, without presumption, say that my reasons will be found in the following pages. I will add that courtesy required that I should offer to the publishers of my original article on this subject the publication of this little volume, which they kindly assumed.

R. G. W.

NEW YORK, October 11, 1880.

PREFATORY.

In the spring of the year 1879 the Messrs. Harper printed and sent to many authors and publishers some interesting and valuable memorandums in respect to reciprocal copyright in the United States of America and Great Britain, accompanied by a request for such suggestions on the subject as those who received these memorandums might deem necessary or useful. Having been favored with copies, I desired to say something again for a cause which awoke my sympathies and enlisted my pen in my earliest manhood, and always seemed to me of even greater importance in its moral and intellectual relations than in those which are merely pecuniary ; but other occupation of my time has prevented me from doing so until now. Yet even at this late day there is evidence—of which Mr. Matthew Arnold's article in the London *Fortnightly Review* is a conspicuous sample—that interest in the question is not diminished.

"The American View of the Copyright Question," which forms the first part of this little book, was published under that title in the London *Broadway Magazine* for May, 1868. I may be pardoned, perhaps, for relating the circumstances under which it was written.

When Mr. Alexander Macmillan, the head of

the London publishing house of Macmillan & Company, was in New York (in the year 1867, I believe), during a visit with which he favored me, I had the pleasure of bringing to his attention the view of the question which is set forth in that article. This view, he said, was quite new to him ; and he deemed it of sufficient importance and interest to ask me to write an article embodying it for *Macmillan's Magazine*. I consented, and at my earliest leisure for such a purpose—in December of that year—I wrote the first part of the article ; but being interrupted, I laid it aside unfinished. Early in the spring of 1868 I was favored by Messrs. Routledge & Son, of London, through their New York agent, Mr. Blamire (with whom I had had no previous conversation tending to such an end), with a request to write for the *Broadway Magazine*, which they then published, an article setting forth to British readers the views and feelings upon this question which prevailed in this country. The request was accompanied with such an offer as to what Armado calls remuneration—which was not in this case, as Costard says, " the Latin word for three farthings"—that it at once excited in me a wish to accept their proposal. I informed them of my pre-engagement, but said that I thought that Mr. Macmillan would release me from it, without which release the article must be his. This, however, he did, and, as I have mentioned before, the article was published in the *Broadway* in May, 1868.

In consequence of a misapprehension of my wishes, the article appeared without my name.

Feeling sure that many readers of the *Broadway* were entirely ignorant of me, I made a particular request that it should be mentiond that it was an "American" author who presented this view of copyright. The editor of the *Broadway* was absent when the manuscript and its accompanying letter arrived in London ; and his *locum tenens*, misapprehending my point, published the article simply as " by an American author."

These facts are mentioned here because in this article the " American" view of the question of copyright in the two countries was the first set forth. That view has since then been presented to the British public by others, most notably, however, by Mr. William H. Appleton, the head of the well-known publishing house of D. Appleton & Company, who some three years and more afterward (October, 1871) repeated it in a letter published in the London *Times*, and by Mr. S. S. Conant in an article in *Macmillan* for June, 1879. The letter, coming from a prominent New York publisher, and appearing in the leading newspaper of the world, attracted much attention. The magazine article skilfully deepened the impression produced by the former. In neither, however, was any material addition made to what had been previously set forth on the subject in the anonymous article, " The American View of the Copyright Question," in which, however, much was said which it did not suit the purpose of either Mr. Appleton or Mr. Conant to repeat.

To that article (which is here reprinted with no other changes than such as I should have made had I seen the proof) I have added a postcript, in which some needed information is given in regard to the proceedings before the Joint Committee of Congress in February, 1872, some errors which seem to have prevailed in regard to a part of those proceedings are corrected, and some additional considerations of the question itself are presented. The subject is in itself a very simple one ; but it seems, as a practical question, to be hopelessly, although wrongfully, entangled with others.

THE AMERICAN VIEW OF THE COPYRIGHT QUESTION.

THE question is as to the copyright of British authors in the United States. For notwithstanding the ingenious use of the converse of this question by a writer in a late number of the *Atlantic Monthly*, the copyright of "American" authors in the British dominions is a matter of such small importance to either people that it would have no appreciable influence upon the action of either Government.* Abstract right is the same in each case; but a clear apprehension that international copyright, as a subject of legislation in the United

* I have unfortunately lost the name and the date of the journal from which the following paragraph is taken; but none the less may it be accepted as setting forth correctly the facts to which it refers.

" English importations of American books, unlike English importations of American gold, bear but a very slender ratio to the books that come from England to the United States. By returns just completed of the exports and imports we find, according to Messrs. Sampson Low, Son & Marston's *Monthly Bulletin*, that the whole value of American books imported into England during last year (1867) was £7522, or nearly £3000 in the year less than the amount of books imported from *Holland* / while the amount exported of English books to the United States during 1867 was £160,311, being rather better than one fourth of the whole value of the books exported to all parts of the world during the year."

States, is not a mere question of the rights of authors, is the first condition necessary to the understanding of this matter. The view of it which I shall here present is, I believe, that which is taken by those whom the question chiefly concerns in the United States, and which therefore cannot fail to be the one which, in the long run at least, will control the action of Congress.

According to my observation this view has never yet been laid before the public of either country, writers upon the subject having treated it chiefly, if not wholly, as a question of the rights of British authors and the consequent duty of " American" publishers and the " American" people.   If this were all, the question would have been set at rest long ago by legislation. securing the copyright of the British author in the United States.   The lack of such legislation is not caused by any unwillingness to pay the British author for the right of reading his book.   The " American" public would as willingly pay copyright money to Mr. Froude as to Mr. Motley, to Mr. Tennyson as to Mr. Bryant or Mr. Longfellow, to Mr. Dickens as to Mr. Lowell.   Yankees may make sharp bargains in the way of trade (so far have they deteriorated from their English original), but they are not mean, nor are they close in small matters ; and the ten or fifteen or twenty-five cents a volume which an international copyright law would add to the cost of a British author's book published in the United States is not a matter as to which they would give any thought, except to be glad that the money went into the author's pocket.

The difficulty in the way is no wish to spoil the British author ; but a dread, and a well-founded dread, of the rivalry of the British manufacturer. Briefly the refusal of copyright in the United States to British authors is, in fact, although it is not so avowed, a part of the " American" protective system.

Simply, of itself, could there be a clearer, plainer matter than this one of copyright? A man invents, after long effort and many failures, a kind of wheelbarrow, serviceable, handy, labor-saving. If you would honestly use the fruit of his time, his labor, and his inventive faculty, you must pay him his price for it. Another man, with much expenditure of time and money, in the culture of what faculty of thinking and thought-utterance he may have been born with, produces, after long brooding and sore travail, a book, which is not only his production, but his child—a part of himself—brought forth from himself—a something to the making of which he has given not only the needful labor but the material. What substance and life there may be in it are not only his but himself. If you use that book, not having paid him his price therefore, can you afterward meet him, or can you behold your own unnatural face in a glass, without blushing ? Is the laborer worthy of his hire, and the creator —he who is both laborer and that which is labored upon—unworthy ? With him who denies, or hesitates about this right, it is necessary to begin at the beginning, and do one of two things—either civilize him up to the point at which he can apprehend a right to that which may be neither seen nor touched—a right incorporeal, or dispute with him upon the righteousness of the command, "Thou shalt not steal."

All this seems plain enough ; but unfortunately for the wholesome conclusion to which it tends, an author's—a native author's—copyright rests neither in Great Britain nor in the United States upon this simple, solid ground.   In equity it rests there ; and so it does at common law.   But since the passage of that accursed statute of Queen Anne, known in the reports as " 8 Anne, cap. 19," the courts and the lawyers have assumed that an author's right in his copy exists in virtue of that Act, or of some one framed upon it, by which, for the gracious encouragement of learning, copyright—that is, a right in his copy, his book—was conferred upon and vested in the author.   Now, if this assumption is well grounded, if it be true that an author's right to say upon what terms people shall have copies of his books, is born of a statute, the British author has no ground of complaint that his books are printed and sold in the United States without profit to him, and without his consent, because in that case he has suffered no wrong.   Both countries have the same English common law ; but British statute law can confer no rights in the United States.   It is a maxim of law that there is no wrong without a remedy.   To turn this maxim round and say, " Here is no remedy, therefore there has been no wrong," might in some cases make the judges stare.   But where a right exists in virtue of a statute, there is of necessity a remedy ; and if copyright exists only in virtue of some statute,

then what need of words to show that where copyright is set at naught and cannot be enforced there
has been no wrong ? If copyright is a creation of
statute law, and the British author and the
British publisher get all that is given by the law,
under which the one writes and the other pub-
lishes, and in virtue of which they claim payment,
then they have all that is theirs. Whatever may
go on beyond the reach of an Act of Parliament,
it cannot touch their rights. If they receive any
more money than comes to them lawfully in virtue
of a right created by law, and which was one of
the chief conditions upon which they undertook
their risk, that more is sheer overplus—a windfall,
gift of the gods, or whatever one may please to
call some bounty that comes we know not exactly
whence or why, but goes we know exactly whither.
What is true in this respect of British authors and
publishers is, of course, equally true of their
" American" brothers and rivals.

But what man of common-sense and single eye
does not see that the assumption of the lawyers is
absurd, monstrous ?—does not see that an author's
right in the use of his works is not statutory ; that
copyright is not created by Act of Parliament or
Act of Congress ? That statute of Queen Anne of
blessed memory created no right ; it destroyed :
it conferred nothing ; it restricted : it did not give ;
it took away. For, as we have already seen, copyright is chiefly among all rights of property a natural right, one that in the very nature of things per-
tains to the maker of the copy, the author.

That a man's thoughts are his own cannot be

disputed, and, like the plainest truths, it can hardly be proved. But they cannot be even possessed by or come to the knowledge of another, unless he communicates them. Does he lose his right of property in them by putting them upon paper? This is not a question of opinion ; it is a question of fact. He puts his manuscript into his drawer, and there it is his exclusive possession, and in his exclusive knowledge—a thing quite out of reach of all other men, except in a country where it may be lawful and usual to break open a man's inclosure, and take his private papers, to your own or to the public benefit. Does he give up his right in it by allowing you to read it, or to make a copy for your own benefit? No ; for however it may be with regard to the spontaneous fruits of nature, the products of human industry, which are the results of labor and contrivance, are owned by a right which must be respected, unless it has been expressly and openly renounced. The writer of a manuscript can fix the conditions upon which it may be used by other persons. Those conditions may be unwise and unkind ; they cannot be unjust, for a man may do what he will with his own ; nor can they be reasonably disputed. He says to the public, " You wish to have the pleasure or the instruction to be derived from the reading of my book. Then, do you, through your Government, secure to me the receipt of a certain proportion of the money for which each copy may be sold, and I will print my book and publish it ; otherwise, back goes my copy into my drawer, or here it goes into the fire !"

Circumstances, common-sense, and an ordinary knowledge of the world may be relied upon to procure for the public the reading of his book without the payment of an exorbitant price to the author ; for, by insisting upon the latter, he would defeat his own interests. Without profitable sale, the book is useless to him as a means of getting a return for his labor. This obvious condition of the case was well made, by Mr. Justice Aston, of the King's Bench, an all-sufficient answer to the argument gravely put before that court—and which is still sometimes heard—that an author, by publication of his book, makes the copy common. In other words, the act necessary to making a book useful and profitable to its author is construed to be destructive of his property in the results of his labor ! Surely such an argument is worthy only of men too uncivilized, or too dull-brained, to see that man may sell the use of a thing without selling the thing itself ; or part with a certain right in it without giving up all his rights ; and that an author, in publishing and selling his book, sells to each buyer a certain use only of the book. He sells the paper, the print, and the binding absolutely, but the book conditionally —that is, he sells the volume, and the use of it, but not the copy. He does not, by publication, openly renounce his natural right in the fruits of his time, his thought, and his labor, without which open renunciation all such natural rights are presumed to be reserved and retained.*

---

* " Barbeyrac, Notes on Puffendorf." Maugham, p. 10.

This right in his copy he *can* sell, give, or bequeath. Unless he can do this with it, it is not his; he is not in its full possession; he has merely the usufruct of his work, a life interest, or an interest more or less limited. To say which, with regard to that which a man has not only produced by labor, but has made, as no man ever makes a ship or a house, or a bale of cotton, is absurd, and, more, it is shameful. An author clearly has a natural right to sell all that he owns. This is no privilege, or peculiar right of his; he has it in common with all other men. He has, therefore, the natural right to sell, or to transfer for any consideration whatever, his absolute control over his copy. The person to whom it is transferred, having acquired all the author's rights, can transfer them to another, and he in his turn to another, and so forth, as long as there is anything to be transferred. So it is with a house or a ship that a man has built; and why it should not be so with a book that he has made no one can say, or at least has hitherto said, except for reasons that invalidate the possession of all property. There comes a time when the house and the ship deteriorate in value, and finally become so worthless that there is nothing in them worth buying; and so it would be with the copyright of a book. But then there are some books that seem to be of immortal worth. Therefore, let him who owns them profit by them, as if he owned a noble, imperishable house. But this profit will not then go to the author. What if it do not? Did the Duke of Rutland build Belvoir Castle? The conclusion is that copyright, if it is not created and conferred by statute, is a natural, absolute, and perpetual right. That it existed, and in the nature of things must have existed, before the making of any law upon the subject, we have seen, I trust, with sufficient clearness. But let us now see what the statute of Anne is, what it pretended to do, and what was the author's relation to his copy before the passing of that Act, and let us consider the last point first.

The common law of England recognized the natural, absolute, and perpetual right of the author in his copy ; and this right was transferred by him, and bought and sold without limitation, until the Act of Queen Anne became British law upon this subject. Books were entered by their titles and their authors' names upon the " Stationers' Register" as belonging to certain persons ; and if these persons sold them to others, the transfer was made upon that register. The register and the transfer made the person recorded as the owner of the book its legal proprietor, with the sole right of printing it ; and the duration of that right was without limitation, expressed or implied. The business of authors, and especially of stationers (as publishers and booksellers were then called), was conducted upon this recognized practice of the trade, this acknowledged right at common law. This custom was proved in the case of Millar *v.* Taylor, for the violation of the copyright of Thomson's " Seasons," which was tried in 1769, and in a special verdict the jury found :

" That before the reign of her late Majesty Queen Anne, it was usual to purchase from au-

thors the perpetual copyright of their books, and
to assign them from hand to hand for valuable considerations, and to make the same the subject of
family settlements, for the provision of wives and
children."*

So much for the notion that copyright is not a
natural, but a statutory right—a right created by
Act of Parliament, which has but recently been seriously put forth.   Sir Thomas Clarke, Master of the
Rolls, said, in 1761, "It is not necessary to determine whether authors had a property in their works
before the reign of Queen Anne.   If they had not,
it was a reproach to the law."   But it is clear that
they had this right.   What the Queen Anne Act
did (under the pretence of the encouragement
of learning, by securing copyright to authors and
their representatives, and enabling them to enforce
those rights) was to restrict, diminish, and limit the
rights of authors in their books, to lay burdens
upon them, and even to control the prices which
they should ask for the fruit of their own labors.
The title of the Act is, "An Act for the Encouragement of Learning, by vesting the copies of
Printed Books in the Authors, or purchasers of
such copies during the times therein mentioned."
Remembering that the copies (that is, property in
the copies) were already vested in the authors by
natural right, and at common law in perpetuity,
and considering that the first section of this law
assumed to confer upon the author of a book, or
upon his representative, the sole right and liberty

* Maugham, p. 16.

of printing such book " for the term of twenty-one years" in certain cases, and in others, " for the term of fourteen years, *and no longer*," we see that this Act gave nothing in the way of copyright, and took away much. It gave something, in making it easier for the author or the publisher to enforce his right, which from the loose and piratical practices of the trade was subject to depredation, against which it had long been difficult for him to protect himself.

This liability to robbery was the only need for legislation upon the subject, so far as " the encouragement of learning" was concerned. Parliament might as well for the encouragement of building have passed an Act providing that every man who built a house should have an undisputed right to live in, rent, or sell it for fourteen years, and no longer. But, in addition to this curtailment and restriction of the property which the author had in his book by natural right and at common law, the Act required every bookseller to sell his books at a price not deemed " too high and unreasonable" by the Lord Archbishop of Canterbury, the Lord Chancellor, and ten other dignitaries of the realm, either one of whom could, upon complaint and after hearing, compel the bookseller to reduce his price to one that seemed just and reasonable to the dignity aforesaid, and to pay the costs of the proceeding. It also provided that nine copies, on the best paper, of every book published should by given by the author and the publisher to the libraries of certain Universities and Faculties, in default of which the copyright should fail, and the bookseller should be fined.   All copyright laws in Great Britain and the United States are mere modifications of this beautiful and beneficent enactment of Queen Anne's day, which, for the encouragement of learning, diminished the author's rights, and laid burdens upon him and his business partner, the publisher.   One copy of each book only has been demanded hitherto in the United States—that deposited as the book of which copyright is claimed.   But some years ago Congress passed an Act requiring a copy to be given to its own library, in default of which the author loses his copyright : a most unrighteous act. Upon what pretence can Congress go to Mr. Longfellow and say, Give us a copy of each one of your books, or you shall have no property in the other copies.

But all this is in keeping.   If Parliament and Congress do really bestow upon authors the right to the enjoyment of the fruit of their labors, then Parliament and Congress, of course, may make the conditions of their gift, or, be it remembered, they may refuse the gift altogether, and on any terms whatever ; and if the author's right in his copy is merely statutory, then the British author has no grounds of complaint that his books are printed without profit to him in the United States, because there British statutes have no force, and there no rights can exist by Act of Parliament.

The remedy for all this confusion and wrong is a simple one.   No legislation is needed—that is, none of a positive character ; no act for the encouragement of learning, of which sort of remedy we have had quite enough already.   Let Parliament and Congress simply repeal in ten words all copyright laws, and the British author's right to his book in the United States, and the " American" author's to his in Great Britain, would be as absolute and as defensible as Sir Edward Cunard's is in one of his steamers, whether it be in New York or Liverpool ; and if it were deemed necessary to restrict the duration of copyright (although the necessity of the restriction is not easy to be discovered), there might be added to the few words of repeal a few others to the effect that, for the benefit of the buyers of books, and to encourage the art of reading, no author's right in his copy shall exist for a longer period than sixty years, or during his own life and that of his heir or heirs-at-law living at the time of his death. Until this step or its equivalent is taken, and the author's right is recognized as one not created, but modified and restricted by statute law, British authors in the United States, and " American" authors in Great Britain, can have no standing, no claim based on right, but only an appeal *in misericordiam* to the compassion of the legislature of either country.

What hope is there that copyright will be given to British authors in the United States, either as alms or as a right ? Very little, in my opinion, although there is now a " movement" for it, and it is understood that a bill will be brought in. The bill may be brought in, and may become a law ; but bills have been brought in before, and there have been movements for international copyright, but there is as yet no law. The nature of the opposition of the United States to an international copyright law has, however, been very much misrepresented to British readers, because it has been so much misunderstood by British writers. The facts of the case are monstrously distorted ; the motives really at work being to British eyes, it would seem, quite invisible.

It has been recently said, for instance, in a very influential quarter in England, that " certain publishers of New York regularly reprint every novel published in England." There could not be a wilder assertion, or one wider from the mark. The publishers of New York would not publish all the novels published in England, or half of them, if the authors would pay for putting them in type—that is, they would not be at the expense of the mere paper, press-work, and binding for the returns, without any deduction for copyright. By doing so they would certainly lose money.

New York publishers print only a very few of the best and the most popular novels published in England ; and of these they calculate to sell large editions at about one fifth of the London prices. It would be within bounds to say that ten times as many novels are published in London every year as are published in New York, including the productions of both British and " American" authors. This and the assertion in the same quarter, that " for one American book stolen in England, one thousand English books are stolen in America," is mere " tall talk"—of the tallest kind. The latter statement may, however, be the result, not of a taste for hyperbole—who would presume to sus-

pect the " Thunderer" of a proneness to exaggera-
tion !—but of ignorance of the fact that many books
by " American" authors are " stolen" by British
publishers in a way which robs the " American"
author not only of his copyright, but of his reputation. They are issued without his name, and
are voided of whatever would tell of their origin.
Even a man so widely known as Henry Ward
Beecher has been subjected to this treatment.
Equally untrue, with the added wrong of injustice,
is the charge that " American" authors " could en-
dure to see the spoliation of their professional
brethren in England, but when their own property
is handed over to be plundered they begin to see
the matter in a totally different light." " American" authors have never been indifferent to the
right and wrong of this question.* They have
always, those of them who did not profess the peril-
ous art of political economy, insisted upon the
unqualified right of the British author to payment for his book in the United States. This
charge is quite as untrue as the kindred one
which I first denied, that the " American" reading
public is unwilling to pay the British author for his
copyright.

What, then, is the difficulty in the way of that
which seems to be admitted on all sides to be the
simple, straightforward course of justice? It is
this—that the admission of the British author to
the unqualified control of his book would secure

---

* See evidence of this in the postscript. The Copyright Association included every man of letters of any note in the United States,
and a few of the publishers.

the " American" market to the British publisher,
which, of course, is what the British publisher
desires.

Now, not only are American publishers opposed
to this, but, what is much more important, all the
paper-makers, the type-founders, the ink-makers,
the binders, and the printers, masters and men,
every one of whom has a vote, and is a " constit-
uent" of some member of Congress, protest with all
their might against it, and demand protection
against the British manufacturer.

Looking at the subject from their own self-inter-
ested point of view, they are right ; for if the British author were admitted to unqualified copyright
in the United States, and with him, of course, his
business partner, the British publisher, all the
crafts which live by book-making would suffer so
greatly and so hopelessly that many of our book
factories and printing-offices would be shut before three years were over. For although books
are generally published in London and Edinburgh
in a style and at a price which places them out of
the reach of the general book-buying public in the
United States, yet the same books could not be
published in New York, Boston, or Philadelphia
at anything like the same · prices, even at the
" American" publisher's rate of profit, which is
much lower than that of the British publisher ; and
when the latter does publish a cheap book, he has
so much advantage over his " American" rival that
he can send his book to New York, pay freight,
charges, a duty of thirty per cent, and commis-
sions, and yet largely undersell the " American"

publisher, let the latter do what he will, free as he is of all these expenses.

" Free trade !" said a well-known Massachusetts printer in my hearing : " yes, I am for free trade. I want the London printer to start fair with me on this side of the water ; then I am not afraid of him. That's what I call free trade. Any other kind of trade I go into with my hands and feet tied together. Much freedom there is in that for me !" He touched the point, which is the protection of American labor at high wages against British labor at low wages. If the book marts of the United States were thrown open to British authors and publishers, the result would be that the " Americans" would not only have most of their books written, but nearly all of them printed and bound for them, in England and Scotland. Cheapness—whatever the quality of the manufacture—would insure the latter ; and as the British and " American" people are the same in race and language, and therefore in literature, the former would be an inevitable consequence of the latter. This is not mere speculation, but a conclusion from notorious facts. For instance, I know one rich publishing house in the United States that would like to publish an edition of Shakespeare's works in one handy volume, which would surely be received with favor ; but the market is absolutely closed to them by two editions handsomely printed and neatly bound in London, which are sold in thousands all over the United States at one dollar and a half in " greenbacks," notwithstanding freight and high duties--a price which would hardly pay here the first cost of the unbound sheets. Shakespeare, indeed, pure and simple, is free of copyright ; but add to this price an author's percentage of copyright, and the difference would not be worth the "American" publisher's consideration in entering the field of competition.

The result of this condition of things is a policy which, if it ever admits the British author to copyright in the United States, will rigidly exclude the British publisher, even from the " American" market that he now commands, which, as he well knows, is very considerable. That is, every book by a British author published in the United States will be required to be manufactured there, and published by a citizen ; and copies printed in Europe or Canada will not be admitted, even under an enormous duty, but will be absolutely excluded.

The only Copyright Bill that ever was received in the House of Representatives with even a semblance of favor—and it was but a semblance—was one brought in by Mr. Morris, of Pennsylvania, just ten years ago.* This Bill, which is now before me, provided—1st, that every book, map, musical composition, or what not, claiming the benefit of the Act, should be "printed and published in the United States, by a citizen of the United States ;" 2d, that the book should be "published and printed in the United States within one month after its publication in the country of which its author is a citizen ;" 3d, that if an author " does not choose to print another edition, then the work

* That is in 1858; this having been written and published in 1868.

may be imported or reprinted by any one, free from the penalties of the Act ;" 4th, that if the foreign author or publisher, or any person not a citizen of the United States, should import copies of the book into the United States for sale, the copyright should be forfeited ; 5th, that periodicals and magazines should be excluded from the benefit of the Act ; 6th, reciprocity.

This Bill did not pass, nor, I believe, get out of committee ; but there was a chance of its passage, so far as Congress was concerned ; and there was less outside opposition to it than had ever been known before in regard to a Bill of its kind. It will be seen that, so far as payment to the British author was concerned, the Bill was without limit or condition, but that it rigidly excluded the British publisher and printer from the "American" market, and not only so, but deprived the British author of all control over his own work, except that he was allowed to make a contract with "a citizen of the United States" for its publication or its republication in the United States within a certain brief period. This was to prevent him from saying that his book should not be published at all, for the trifling reason, for example, that he had modified his views, and wished to re-write his book, thereby in the first instance depriving "American" printers of work, and in the second putting "American" publishers to expense for his unreasonable vagaries. In a word, the Bill was as radically unjust to the author as the statute of Queen Anne was, because, like that, it failed to recognize and respect the author's natural and absolute right in the product of his own labor. If any international copyright law is ever passed by Congress, it can hardly fail to contain all these provisions.* Nor would the mass of British authors profit by such a Bill. Only a favored few would receive copyright money, and the rest would fail to gain even the reputation which is gratifying to all, and which in the end does have money value. The result would be that the wealthiest publishing houses in the United States— a very small number, half a dozen, all told—would publish and pay copyright for the works of a few British authors of high reputation and great popularity. The works of others it would not be to their interest to publish and pay copyright for; and these, not being published by a citizen of the United States within the limited time, would be open to any one's use without any payment whatever. With free trade we shall have just international copyright—that is, copyright without any law upon the subject. And free trade will come when, by changes in the labor market, the cost of manufacturing is about the same on both sides of the water—that is, when, for the objects for which

* While this article has lain half finished on my table [1868] a Bill has been framed, but has not yet been brought in, providing for international copyright. Some people have hopes that it will become a law. It is almost identical with Mr. Morris's, above described, but it extends the time during which a book must be published in the United States after publication in another country to three months. Like Mr. Morris's, it excludes the British publisher and printer from the markets of the United States in regard to all copyrighted books, and it deprives the British author of the control of his own work.

it is now desired, by those who do desire it, free trade will be worthless ; and they, like others before them who have at last attained their ends, will cry, Too late, too late !

POSTSCRIPT.

———

THE foregoing presentation of the " American" view of the copyright question having been published in 1868, not only in the *Broadway Magazine,* but, in the same year, by the Copyright Association, the subject continued to be languidly discussed until three or four years afterward, when Mr. Appleton's repetition in the London *Times* (1871) of the view presented ~~of~~ this article and the commission (1872) of the subject of international copyright by Congress to a joint committee of both Houses (that on the Library) directed public attention again somewhat to the subject. I say somewhat ; for it is not to be concealed that the general public takes very little interest in this question of international copyright. They are quite willing to pay the foreign writer, they are willing to pay any writer, for his work ; but they would like to pay him and have done with it, and not be " bored and bothered" by the discussion of abstract rights. They regard it as a matter which concerns publishers and authors only ; and they wonder why those whom it chiefly concerns don't settle it fairly and quietly among themselves.*

---

* In all the earlier stages of civilization, whatever a man owned he kept in his custody, and could defend *vi et armis* if need be. As civilization, and security, its attendant, grew, he took his money

When it was known that the Congressional Joint Committee was to take the subject of international copyright into consideration, and had sent out invitations to authors, publicists, and publishers to appear before them and present their views of the question, some preparation was made on all sides for the occasion. The publishers went into consultation to draft a Bill to be presented to the committee. This Bill was adopted by the majority and presented at Washington in February, 1872, by Mr. William Appleton. It was received with marked disfavor by all respectable organs of public opinion* The draft of another Bill was presented at

out of his chest and kept it in the bank. He became the owner of indivisible shares in all sorts of enterprises, and of books which were read all over the world. His money in bank, and his shares in railroads and canals, and his rights under trusts, jurisprudence and public opinion speedily took charge of, because these were kinds of property of which everybody felt he might himself any day become possessed. But property in books is a kind of property which not one man in a million ever dreams of possessing. The owners of it have always been, and will always be, a small and peculiar class, and the property a peculiar property, and therefore the failure of society to protect them has not seemed likely to endanger the security of other classes of possessions, and it is consequently very difficult to get society to trouble itself about their special interests.— *The Nation*, February 15, 1872.

From the N. Y. Evening Post, January 30, 1872.

* " Doubtless the gentlemen, deservedly eminent in their own business, who have prepared this bill, are sincere in believing that it will establish an international copyright, and in expecting that the old friends of that great measure will approve and support their action. But they have mistaken their way, and ought to know it before they go astray further. Their bill is not only not an international copyright bill, but it is in all essential respects the opposite of such a bill. If made a law, it would put backward for

the same time.   This Bill is said by Mr. Conant in his well-known " Macmillan" article to have been presented by Mr. Charles Astor Bristed ; and he mentions it again as " Mr. Bristed's measure," saying, not quite correctly, as we shall see, that it

ιιαιχ / a generation the progress of just and liberal ~~news~~ on this subject, and no intelligent friend of international copyright can consent to it.

*　　*　　*　　*　　*　　*　　*　　*

" It is a mere pretence to call it an ' International Copyright.' bill.   A law whose design is to protect literary property ought at least to pay some regard to the views and interests of authors, but this bill is drawn solely for the benefit of our publishers, to increase the ' protection ' they already have against foreign competition.

*　　*　　*　　*　　*　　*　　*　　*

" Again, it is the common practice in Europe for an author to rewrite and improve his book in each successive edition, while here nearly every volume is stereotyped. Thus the common American editions of such books as Alford's 'Greek Testament,' first volume, Lyell's 'Principles of Geology,' Grove's 'Correlation of the Physical Forces,' Grote's 'History of Greece,' still sold here every day, are really stereotyped reprints of old editions, which have been superseded in England, for from five to twenty years, by new and improved ones.   Now, the bill in question protects the reprint by absolutely excluding all foreign editions, so that in each of these, and hundreds of similar instances, it would make it simply impossible for anybody in the United States to obtain access to the latest discoveries and the maturest views of European men of letters and of science.

" All these faults are inherent in the bill, and cannot be removed by amendments, for the central idea of it is utterly wrong in principle."

From the N. Y. World, February 2, 1872.

" The proposed act to grant a copyright to foreign authors is curiously misnamed ; it should have been entitled 'An act to place the reading public at the mercy of American publishers.' By its provisions, if one of the said American publishers deem it for his own advantage to do so, he may purchase the copyright of a foreign work and thereby prevent the importation of a single com-

attracted little attention. But it was not presented by Mr. Bristed ; nor was it in any sense his measure. He had no part either in the drafting of it or in its presentation.

When the sitting of the Joint Committee of Con-

peting copy ; but if, on the other hand, he find it more lucrative to steal he has only to decline negotiations with the author in order to obtain full liberty to reprint as heretofore. The simple fact that few American publishers are known by name to foreign authors, while all European authors of repute are known to American publishers, would alone suffice to render the working of such an act altogether one-sided. Why can we not have a genuine author's copyright, recognizing the writer's absolute title to that property which he creates? To steal an author's article in manuscript would be felony ; to deny his right to keep it private would be preposterous. Why, then, should any one be allowed to steal it with impunity after it is printed, or to dictate the conditions under which he may multiply copies of it ? Authorship either gives ownership to literary property, or it does not. If it do, such property belongs to the author as absolutely as money or merchandise of other kinds, and should be as fully protected by law, whether municipal or international. If it do not, all legislation concerning copyright is needless and unjust."

From the N. Y. Tribune, February 8, 1872.

" Profoundly convinced that ' the laborer is worthy of his hire that you can in no other way obtain the fruits of another's exertions cheaper than by fairly buying and honestly paying for them— we beg Congress to pass some bill recognizing and protecting the right of an author to compensation from those who shall see fit to use his works.

" We know not how to enforce the author's claim more forcibly than by simply stating it. If that great primal interdict—' Thou shalt not steal '—does not reach this case, we see not how it can apply to any act whatever. Four brothers set to work : one of them grows corn ; a second makes shoes ; a third breeds sheep and produces wool ; the fourth makes histories or poems. You are at perfect liberty to use none of these ; you are *not* at liberty to use any but the last without paying therefor. Why the exception ? If

gress was announced, and its invitations, before
mentioned, were issued, I received one of the
latter, and having been informed of the movement of the publishers, consulted the Chairman of

(like us) you don't know, ask Congress to pass an international
copyright law at this session. And to the end that you may ask
intelligently, consider the discussion by Professor Youmans, and
the kindred information presented this morning on our sixth page."

From the Evening Post, February 3, 1872.

" It has been a long and tedious work to make our lawmakers
willing to confer upon all authors the right to their own work ; but
Congress seems at last to be coming to the conviction that justice
and the public intelligence require it of them. The Joint Committee of Congress now have the subject under consideration, and
the Executive Committee of the Copyright Association adopted
yesterday the following draft of an international copyright bill,
which they will offer to Congress at once :

" This bill, or something equivalent to it, ought to become law.
It is simple, clear, comprehensive, and just ; just to all parties directly or indirectly interested in this subject. It secures to foreign
authors and artists no right which is not already recognized as
belonging to our own ; it provides for a reciprocal grant to our
authors of similar rights in other countries, and by its last section
it wisely and considerately gives time in which all persons interested in publishing may make such changes in their business
(should any be necessary) that they may suffer from no sudden dis-
arrangement of their plans.

" The bill is presented by a committee of which we observe that
Henry W. Longfellow, Dr. Lieber, George W. Curtis, Dr. S. Irenæus Prime, President Barnard, of Columbia College, Richard
Grant White, and William C. Bryant are members ; and acting with
these men of letters we find such publishers as Messrs. George P.
Putnam and Henry Holt. It is entirely free from the objections
which we have shown to be fatal to the bills hitherto suggested, and
especially to that prepared by the New York publishers' committee ;
and, once adopted, it promises to be a final settlement of the whole
question, to the satisfaction of literary men as well as of the public conscience."

the Executive Committee of the Copyright Association, Dr. Prime, and by his instructions called a meeting of that Committee for the purpose of drafting a Bill to be submitted to the Committee of Congress on the part of the Association. Several adjourned meetings of the Executive Committee were held, at which the subject was very thoroughly discussed. Members submitted to the Committee independent and different drafts of a Bill, some of which were long, and made various provisions upon particular points. Finally, however, much consultation resulted in the unanimous decision that there was but one rightful and proper mode of treating the subject, which was the simple reciprocal recognition by the Government of the United States of all rights granted by foreign governments to citizens of the United States ; and a Bill to that effect was by unanimous consent drafted and ordered to be presented to the Committee of Congress on the part of the Association. The Bill and the letter submitting it were as follows :

WASHINGTON, February 12, 1872.

SIR : In pursuance of a resolution of the Executive Committee of the Copyright Association, I have the honor of transmitting herewith a copy of the draft of a Bill to secure authors the right of property in their works, which was adopted by that Committee on the 2d instant for presentation to the Joint Committee of Congress of which you are Chairman.

The Executive Committee of the Copyright Association present this draft, not as embodying or expressing, in their judgment, the principle on which any author's rights of property in his work must rest, but as being the most practicable and acceptable step toward the material recognition of those rights that it can be hoped that Congress may take at the present time, and as one that will not leave unprotected from the injury of sudden derangement any interest, so-called, which may be directly or indirectly involved with the rights in question.

In obedience to instructions, I also append to the draft a list of the officers of the Association by which it is presented.

I am, sir, very respectfully, your obedient servant,

RICHARD GRANT WHITE,

Secretary, etc.

A BILL TO SECURE TO AUTHORS THE RIGHT OF PROPERTY IN THEIR WORK.

Be it enacted by the Senate and House of Representatives in Congress assembled:

1. All rights of property secured to citizens of the United States of America by existing copyright laws of the United States are hereby secured to the citizens and subjects of every country the government of which secures reciprocal rights to citizens of the United States.

2. This act shall take effect two years from the date of its passage.

LIST OF OFFICERS.

President, William C. Bryant ; *Vice-Presidents*, Henry W. Longfellow, George H. Boker, W. Gilmore Sims, Francis Lieber, George William Curtis, Horace Greeley, F. A. P. Barnard ; *Recording Secretaries*, Charles Astor Bristed, Anson D. F. Randolph ; *Corresponding Secretary*, Joseph Parton ; *Treasurer*, Henry Ivison ; *Executive Committee*, S. Irenæus Prime, George P. Putnam, S. S. Cox, Henry Holt, Charles Scribner, Edmund C. Stedman, Richard Grant White.*

This letter, as well as the Bill, had the approval of the Executive Committee ; but neither the Bill nor the letter, which were prepared in New York, were seen before their presentation by Mr. Bristed, who was living in Washington in ill health. The delegates from the Association were Mr. Henry Holt, the Hon. S. S. Cox, and R. Grant White. The first, however, did not, I believe, accept his appointment. Mr. Bristed was present at the meeting of the Congressional Committee by invitation as a man of letters who had taken an interest in the question of copyright. This will appear by his own letter given below. Mr. Cox was at Washington. I was also present. My seat was next the Chairman and facing the delegation opposed to the law, which seemed to be largely composed of gentlemen from Philadelphia. A quarter of an hour had not passed before I saw

---

* Of these officers it should be remarked that five are well-nown publishers.

k

that the whole proceeding was merely formal in so far as any consideration of the subject on its merits was concerned ; and some pretence of that I admit that I had been weak enough to expect. But when the gentlemen from Philadelphia spoke, which they did early and often, there was not a word as to the question of justice, right, and truth involved, but simply the setting forth, in effect, of the fact that the speakers represented a business in which a certain number of dollars was invested, which employed a certain number of men, and which had certain connections, and (by implication) controlled so many votes, and that they were opposed to any change in the law. The committee were all plainly with these speakers. After submitting to this for a while, Mr. Bristed rose and poured out his indignation in a speech which, as it was equally true and intemperate, harmed his cause at every sentence—if that could be said to be harmed which was already condemned. Not less disappointed and disheartened, I managed to keep silent ; but telling Mr. Bristed that he might remain if he chose as a puppet, I took the afternoon train for New York. It is needless to say that nothing was done that was really to the professed purpose of the sitting. But there was a consultation and an attempt at compromise, the nature of which is set forth in the following very characteristic letter from Mr. Bristed to Mr. George P. Putnam, of which Mr. Putnam kindly allowed me to take a copy for future use in the Executive Committee of the Copyright Association and which, both parties being no longer living, it seems not now improper to publish as an interesting contemporary record of the *res gestæ* of the occasion :

1325 K STREET, WASHINGTON,
February 14, 1872.

G. P. PUTNAM, ESQ.

DEAR SIR : I do not know what report Messrs. Andrews and White may have made to you or to the Executive Committee ; but there is no harm in my saying something.

Monday morning, the [Congressional] Committee being all there (I think) except Senator Howe, and twenty persons altogether present, permanently, not counting White and Cox, Mr. Andrews spoke for the author's *right.* Mr. Appleton followed for *his* Bill,* but ended by offering to withdraw it and accept *ours,* with one additional clause—viz., that the book should be manufactured here. I then said a few words on the error and danger of always referring to the great book-manufacturers as the only authorities on literary matters. In the afternoon session Hazard, of Philadelphia, attacked the whole principle of copyright, and Sheldon and Youmans defended it, from the Appleton point of view. After the session, having talked with Van Nostrand and Sheldon, and put some questions to Appleton, Andrews and I agreed to accept Appleton's proposition and row in the same boat ; and this we stuck to, though he (or some one) did not use us quite fairly, but put into the draft a fourth arti-

---

* The Bill adopted at the publishers' meeting before mentioned.

cle with some of the originally objectionable conditions about magazine articles, etc.

At Tuesday's session an unprepossessing person,
who called himself a Bostonian and representative
of the people, but evidently represented—— ——*
(who had also introduced a false bill through Senator Sherman) made a "shystering," pettifogging
speech which provoked numerous interruptions
from Andrews, Youmans, and Sheldon. And then
the Committee had had enough of us. My idea
is that *any* bill—that is, any bill that can possibly
work—should be taken to start with—the *premier
pas* — which ~~many~~ receive successive improve-
ments in time. I am sorry to say, however, that
Sir Edward Thornton thinks the English publishers
will defeat the Appleton Bill in England. White
was here at first, but dared not speak—he may
have considered that he spoke by Andrews. † I
hope that you and Holt and the Committee and
the Association, and authors generally, won't think
that I have "gone back on them," or neglected
their interests. I hold that a man should be open
to conviction on the expediency of particular issues, while not renouncing his general principles

[margin: m ay/]

---

* I take the liberty here of omitting a caustic and witty designa-
tion of a well-known publishing house, although it is highly characteristic of the writer. It is not at all to the purpose, nor of any
real importance ; and I know that it injuriously misrepresents the
gentlemen to whom it was applied by my able and highly-esteemed
but strongly-prejudiced and sharp-tongued friend.

† Mr. Andrews appeared as counsel, in the interests of certain
authors. He had called upon me and consulted with me in New
York, and we went on to Washington together. I had not seen
him before, and have not seen him since.

and I am bound to say also that Van Nostrand, Sheldon, and Youmans made out a much better case for the Appleton interest (as we may call it) than I had supposed possible.

Very truly yours, C. A. BRISTED.

Mr. Bristed's hope that the compromise which he assumed to make on the part of the Copyright Association would be accepted with favor was quickly and utterly disappointed. I admit that I deserted my post. But I did so in the interests alike of the cause which I had at heart and of the Association which I had the honor of representing. It seemed clear to me that neither the interests of the one nor the dignity of the other was to be served by countenancing or having anything to do with a proceeding which was such a sham as this appeared to me from the beginning, and ultimately proved. If I had spoken, it must have been either in the bitter and injurious tone of Mr. Bristed's first remarks, or else under a very severe and painful restraint, and with a conviction that if I could have uttered the wisdom of Solon in the accents of Demosthenes, it would have been as vain and futile as the idle wind.

News of the unauthorized compromise (of which I knew nothing) quickly reached New York; and it was received by the leading organs of public opinion there in a manner which it is important to consider, not only in regard to the merits of the question itself, but because it shows the feeling of representative public writers on a subject as to which public feeling in the United States is much misapprehended and has been much misrepresented in Europe. Extracts from the principal articles elicited by this proceeding are given below.*

* *From the N. Y. Evening Post, February* 15, 1872.

"This bill [that of the Copyright Association] meets with vigorous opposition from all publishers from whom it would take away the privilege they now enjoy with impunity of republishing English books without paying for them. But, finding that the sentiment of intelligent men is strongly in favor of recognizing the rights of authors everywhere, some of these gentlemen now bring forward a substitute for the international copyright, insisting that their substitute will protect the property of authors just as well, and will at the same time protect the publishing interests of the nation from the injury they would suffer if British copyrights were extended over this country. Their plan is to extend a copyright to foreign authors on condition that the books protected shall be wholly manufactured in the United States. That is to say, they turn the measure which was designed to recognize the rights of authors into one for establishing a protected monopoly in the hands of publishers. We have already exposed the impolicy and injustice of this condition; and our objections have not been answered.

"It is now reported from Washington that two gentlemen who appeared before the Committee to advocate the international copyright bill have taken it upon themselves to ' withdraw ' that bill, and to join the publishers in supporting their substitute. By what right they could thus, in behalf of the International Copyright Association, have presumed to reverse its official action, and to accept a bill which cannot in any sense be regarded as establishing an international copyright at all, we are not informed. If the gentlemen in question were a majority of the Committee of the Association, there might be some claim of right on their part to act for it, but even then they ought at least to call a meeting of the Association to reconsider its course. But, in fact, *neither of them, we believe, is even a member of the Committee*, nor is it likely that any two members of the Committee would have ventured thus to nullify its matured convictions without consulting Messrs. Longfellow, Curtis, Grant White, Lieber, and other members of the Committee, who had, after two years, during which this same publishers' protective

These extracts—as well as those given previously in regard to the Appleton or publishers' Bill—from the most respectable and influential newspapers in New York, where literary matters and questions of abstract right are looked upon with less interest than they awaken in other communities in the United States, make it clear, first, that in regard to

plan had been before them, unanimously rejected it, and determined to adhere to the simple plan of a truly international copyright.

" We are, therefore, justified in assuming that if the gentlemen who argued for an international copyright before the Library Committee have really changed their minds and accepted the publishers' protective scheme, they have done so on their own account alone, and do not represent the International Copyright Association. And we beg leave to remind that Committee that the Association in question speaks to them by its official action, and asks for the passage of an international copyright law in its simplest, fairest, and most intelligible form. It does not want the question complicated by introducing into the discussion any irrelevant issue. It has no concern itself with the strife between free trade and protection, and demands that copyright shall not be made odious to intelligent men by associating it with extreme protectionist measures.

    *   *   *   *   *   *   *   *

" It may be assumed with confidence that if a real international copyright is ever to be established, the persons to be first considered and consulted are the authors themselves, and not the publishers."

From the N. Y. World, February 13, 1872.

" If Congress and the Committee to whom it has referred the question of copyright choose to consider that question as one of rights, they will arrive at a very different conclusion from the one they will reach if they treat it as a conflict of interests only. Not but what we believe the permanent interests of the American public to coincide with the rights of the case in demanding a real and full copyright. But it is quite as hopeless to expect the average Congressman to rise to an enlarged or statesmanlike view of a question of policy as to expect from him a just decision on a question of copyright legislation the rights of authors are even there regarded as paramount, and next that the proposed compromise by which those rights were to be curtailed in the interests of the manufacturers of books, instead of being received with favor, was rejected with something like indignation.

Since this conspicuous failure in 1872 nothing

ethics. Congressmen have been found to argue, or at least vehemently to assert, that voting is a 'natural right,' who will yet undoubtedly be found to maintain that a man, if he happens to live out of the country, has no right to be rewarded for his labor by those who live in it and use the fruits of that labor. If this latter view prevails, it is difficult to show to those who adopt it, and who believe in the hand-to-mouth sort of legislation which is habitual in Congress, that we ought to pass any international copyright bill at all, or the semblance of any. . . . It may, indeed, be convenient to some publishers, under color of compensating the author, to secure the monopoly of the American market for their own manufactures, and to ask Congress to protect them, not only by duties, as is done now, but by absolute prohibition against competition from abroad, while their 'copyright' protects them from competition at home. But this is an invasion of the book-buyer's right to buy any edition he likes so long as he pays those concerned in providing it. And Congress has certainly no call to protect these publishers from the competition of English editions. The publishers who are willing to grant partial copyright in exchange for absolute monopoly were represented before the Committee yesterday by Mr. Appleton. Those who are averse to any form or pretence of compensating a writer, but boldly advocate stealing his work outright and fighting over the booty, were represented by Mr. Hazard, of Philadelphia. It seems strange that a man should not have more shame than to stand up and read, even *coram* a committee of Congress, 'a lengthy argument and remonstrance' to show the advantages of acquisition by theft over acquisition by purchase. But Mr. Hazard is hardly to be blamed, being a Philadelphia publisher, and so we may charitably presume blinded by his interests, when we remember that Philadelphians who call themselves political economists, and who do not avow

of importance has been attempted in regard to this
question until the present time. But certain
changes have taken place in the business of manufacturing and selling the books of foreign authors
which need not be set forth particularly here,
one result of which is a renewed agitation of the
subject, and an attempt, to which some influential
publishing houses are parties, to procure a treaty

that they are hired advocates, have taken his view of the question
from pure perversity. A third and rational proposition was laid
before the Committee by the 'Copyright Association.' But it is
almost too much to hope that it will even receive serious consideration.

From the N. Y. Nation, February 15, 1871.

" Let us say, in conclusion, that there could not be a more strik-
ing illustration of the way in which people are deceived by names
than the notion that, as long as we do not have to go to Europe
for our printing and binding, we preserve ourselves from colonial
dependence on England in literary matters. The fact is that there
could not be a stronger proof of the depth of that dependence
than the plea put forward by the publishers, that they could not
live if they could not get English copyrights for nothing. Our independence is not secured by getting all our books printed in New
York or Boston, but by getting our thinking done in New York
or Boston. As long as our thinking is done in London and
Paris, we shall be intellectually colonial, no matter where we
do our printing and binding. To secure literary independence,
what is wanted is native thinkers ; and our conviction is that there
is nothing which contributes so much to keep down literature as a
profession in the United States, to make American poets, novelists
and speculators inferior to those in Europe, and to keep the people
of the United States in a condition of mental vassalage to the Old
World, in spite of their political emancipation, as the long refusal
of the nation to give native writers the stimulus, encouragement,
and protection that would come from compelling native publishers
to pay foreign authors for their works. No matter how great the
difficulties which surround honesty, stealing in the long run is never
profitable."

between Great Britain and the United States by which British authors shall be allowed copyright here, if their books are manufactured here by a citizen of the United States in virtue of a contract made within a certain time of their publication in Great Britain. Magazine articles are, however, to be exempted from this qualified legal protection. Having been asked to unite in the attempt to procure the making of such a treaty, I may without unwarranted intrusion of my opinion say that I see two objections to it, one of which is fatal. First, that it is unjust to the British author, and to all authors ; second, that it would be null and void, and would afford no protection either to the British author or to his American publisher.

Upon the question of the right of the author, the advocates of what may be called the Philadelphia theory of negation have recently received support which they are naturally inclined to make the most of. In a recent number of the *Fortnightly Review* Mr. Matthew Arnold discussed this long-vexed question with that somewhat dainty dilettanteism which has become a characteristic trait of his style, otherwise so admirable, so suggestive, and so charming. He considered the subject chiefly from the British author's point of view, but he also examined it in its general relations to literature. What Mr. Arnold says upon such a subject is likely to carry so much weight, and to have so much influence, that I cannot but regret that on this occasion his trumpet has a somewhat more than usually uncertain sound. He is manifestly much dissatisfied with the present condition of the British author's legal right in his literary property ; but he says little that tends to strengthen that right, and nothing that helps to extend it. In fact, he leaves us at the end of his article very much doubting whether he believes that any author, in any country, at home or abroad, has really a right to control the publication of his writings or to receive any of the money that is paid for the privilege of reading them, or that he should have, in the latter respect, any surer or clearer dependence than the " delicacy" of publishers and of readers.

In the consideration of this question in its international aspects, one point is axiomatic. If literary property is rightfully the mere creation of statute law, the publication of a book without the writer's consent in a country the statute laws of which have given him no control over it is not a wrong, whether he be native to that country or foreign ; and the absence of any such statute, although it may be impolitic, is not a wrong to him, whether he be native or foreign. The contrary cannot be maintained without a denial of the position that an author's right of property in his book is rightfully the mere creation of statute law. And if that be the nature of the right, British authors cannot justly complain that their property is " conveyed " from them by Americans who publish their books without first obtaining their consent ; for in that case they can have rightfully no property in their literary work except that which is created for them by British statutes, and when they have received the benefit of those stat-

utes in all the lands in which they run, they have
had all that they may justly ask for, or even expect.

That such is rightfully, or even actually, the nature of a writer's property in his work is, however, not to be admitted, except upon grounds
which would sustain the denial of all property
whatever—of property in anything that can be
made or possessed. There is a way of muddling
this question of literary property and of maundering
about it that is very apt to provoke men of common
sense and common honesty to wrath. Mr. Arnold
(whom I would not for a moment place in the
position of one who would willingly confuse right
and wrong) says, in regard to an author's alleged
natural right in his book, that for him the matter
is simplified by his believing that "men, if they
go down into their own minds and deal quite freely
with their own consciousness, will find that they
have not any natural rights at all." It may be
safely assumed, I think, that most men would
have to go down much farther than to the depths
of their own inner consciousness to find such a
camel to deal with as this strange notion. What
wonder, then, that he says, also, that "there is a
breach of delicacy in reprinting the foreigner's
poem without his consent; there is no breach of
honesty." And he quotes Mr. Farrar as distin-
guishing between that which is "property in
itself" and that which is "not property in itself," a book being of the latter sort; and also Sir
Louis Mallet as insisting that "property arises
from limitation of supply." The latter dictum is
an exquisitely characteristic example of the politico-

economical moonshine which is sometimes cast as light upon plain common-sense subjects.

But as to this question of literary property, it is quite beyond all discussion, upon metaphysical grounds, or upon politico-economical grounds, or, indeed, upon any grounds at all ; for it is simply a matter of fact. At the risk of superfluous repetition, let us briefly set forth again this fact. A man has written a book, and it is in his possession, in his table drawer. It had no existence until he made it and put it there. Now, if you wish to print that book or to read it, how are you going to obtain either privilege except upon such conditions as he may impose ? True, you, in the interest of a general diffusion of intelligence (I believe that is the accepted phrase), and of your own pocket (I believe that is not the accepted phrase), and as a friend of humanity, may in his absence, or with force and arms in his presence, break open his drawer, take out his book, and read it yourself, or print it for others to read who will pay *you* for the privilege of doing so ; just as other friends of humanity break open men's drawers and take from them other things for their own use. But this proceeding is recognized by all civilized Christendom as robbery, and is punished as such. How, therefore, are you to get the writer's manuscript, for whatever purpose, without agreeing to his conditions, unless you forcibly rob him of it ? This is no question of metaphysics or of political science. The book *is his.* He made it, and it is in his possession. You cannot take it away from him or appropriate to yourself the use of it with-

out violence which strikes at the root of all property, and makes it law that

> " They should take who have the power,
> And they should keep who can."

This simply is the fact.   And when, in consideration of this matter of fact, you have complied
with his conditions, and have obtained his consent
that you shall use his book, either to read it yourself, or to copy it with pen or types for others to
read, shall you not be bound by his conditions and
observe your agreement with him?   You can refuse to do so only by what has been known from
time immemorial as fraud.   I take it that not Mr.
Matthew Arnold, nor Mr. Farrar, nor Sir Louis
Mallet would deny this matter of fact or dispute
these conclusions.   Should they do so, I for one,
if I should have the honor of discussing this subject with them, should feel it necessary to settle
first the slight preliminary question whether there
are such distinctions as mine and thine, or right
and wrong, at all.

When, however, an author has consented to the
publication of his work, his property in it has assumed a new form ; it then becomes, not the possession of a book which is the product of his mind
and hand, but something in which he has only a
copyright.   It is a literary property ; and if literary property is rightfully the mere creation of
statute law, then, again, his copyright is justly
concurrent only with the statute by which it is
created.

Now, the difficulty for us with regard to this

question, nationally or internationally, is the assumption by our fundamental law that literary property *is* the mere creation of statute law. The terms of that passage of the Constitution of the United States which gives Congress power over this subject imply that authors have no right in their works independent of statute, and Congress is empowered to give them that right only " for limited times." The just view of this subject has been widely and sadly perverted by the statute of Queen Anne, which, professing to act for "the encouragement of learning," assumed to confer upon authors the exclusive right to print their books for certain limited periods of 21 and 14 years, " and no longer." All that is necessary for the perfect security of authors, either in Great Britain or in the United States, or in both, is the repeal of that statute of Queen Anne, and of that clause in the Constitution, and of all laws founded upon them. No statute upon the subject is necessary ; and the law of man's necessity and that of demand and supply may be surely relied upon to protect any supposed rights of the public to profit by the labors of men of letters.

Mr. Arnold begins his article by admitting that the great Parisian publisher, Michel Levy, was right in his decision that the reading world needed cheap books—a decision his action upon which revolutionized the publishing trade of France, profitably to authors and to publishers ; and he (Mr. Arnold) closes his article with the declaration, " The Americans ought not to submit to our absurd system of dear books ; I am sure that they will not, and as a lover of civilization I should be sorry, although I am an author, if they did."

Without a doubt that is the chief difficulty of this question, which, as I showed twelve years ago, is one not between the American public and the British author, but between American paper-makers, type-founders, printers, and bookbinders on the one hand, and the British publisher on the other. This attitude toward the British publisher and toward his aids—the printers and makers of book materials—must be regarded as wrongful by all who believe, as I do, in freedom of trade as well as in just freedom in everything else. And it should never be forgotten by British authors that their privation of copyright on their works published in this country is the consequence, not of any indifference to their rights by the "American" people, but of a protective system, which seeks to exclude the British publisher from the book market of the United States.

Therefore, if Mr. Arnold supposes, as he seems to suppose, that the difficulty of this question would be overcome by the publication of books in London cheaply, after the manner of Michel Levy —books, as he says, at 3*s*. instead of 6*s*. to 12*s*.— he is, I think, sure to be disappointed, even if the London publishers should follow his suggestion. For this there are two reasons. Such books as he refers to as models of cheapness—those published by Levy and by Charpentier—would not meet the demand, the peculiar demand, in this country for cheap literature. They would not be accepted here as supplying it ; for they do not give enough for the price. Too much is expended on good paper, legible type, and comfortable margins. What is meant in the United States by cheap literature is, books printed on bad, thin paper, with small type, in double columns, so that a London three-volume novel is got into a thin magazine-like compass, and sold for fifty or seventy-five cents. To enjoy this the "American" is quite willing to pay the British author copyright. He would willingly have ten per cent added to the price of the book, and pay it all himself, for the author's benefit. But when he is asked to pass a law which will compel him to buy the British author's book of the British publisher at a price certainly twice and probably three or four times greater than he now pays, and to do that for the benefit, not of the author, but of the British manufacturer, he buttons his pocket and hardens his heart. Moreover, if the British publisher should publish cheap books, the end which he, and it seems Mr. Arnold also, seeks would not by attained. For the London publisher can beat his Boston or his New York rival at cheap publishing " out and out." He can pay duty and freight and sell books here bound in muslin for less than we can lay down the printed sheets for, on equally good paper, and with equally good press-work, as I know, sadly to my cost. Therefore, until the question is decided, not upon the ground of " delicacy," but upon that of an honest recognition of the author's right in his own work, the British author will never be permitted to sell his British-printed book here, however cheap it is. The cheaper the worse.

For the object of those who oppose the granting a complete right of property to authors in their works is not to give the "American" public cheap books, but to secure to "American" book-manufacturers the unrivalled, undisturbed right of publishing in this country the works of British writers. For example, a law which should exclude the books of British writers entirely from republication in the United States would be much more stoutly resisted than any other conceivable law upon the subject. The opponents of complete copyright insist upon the right of reprinting the British author's book, will he nill he, in their own way, at their own time, and at their own price ; but if he will, they are now ready to pay him for his copyright, provided the book in its original form is excluded from the country.

They insist upon the oppressive and economically absurd enactment that, for their benefit, a book addressed to all English-speaking people shall be manufactured twice—once for all the world outside of the United States, and then once more for the people within the United States. Let the British publisher sell the British author's book here even more cheaply than the "American" publisher can afford to sell it, and thus give the "American" public that boon of cheap reading which is held up as invaluable, something worth more to a people than honest dealing, and still these philanthropists say, " No ; we must have the privilege of making and the profit of selling the book in the United States." This attitude toward the producer and the product of labor, which it is sought to sanction and establish by law, is strange and peculiar. An " American" merchant goes to London with his cotton and sells it to whom he pleases, and British law defends him in that right to his property. A British or a French author comes to this country and brings his book. It is his exclusive property. He has the natural and perfect right to it, and to dispose of it to whom and for what he pleases. If the Government makes a law requiring him, if he sells it here, to sell it only to an " American" citizen, it treats the author as it treats no other workman, tradesman, merchant, or importer. It says to the merchant, You may sell your wares to whom you please, Englishman, Frenchman, Jew or Gentile ; but to the author it says, If you wish to sell your wares in this country you must sell them to an " American" publisher. If you let any German or French or English publisher have your book, then it shall be lawful for Harper, or Appleton, or Lippincott to reprint it instantly, and to take to himself all the profit you would otherwise get from your labor. This is putting the author upon a footing entirely distinct from any other dealer. It discriminates *against* literary property. It destroys the value of the author's book as property, and compels him to sell it to parties whom the law selects for him, instead of those whom he selects for himself. The law treats no other workmen or producers in that way. To establish iniquity by law is injurious to nations as to individuals ; and it is iniquitous to withhold from the author the shield of that law which defends all other producers.

The advancement of our own branch of English literature would not be the only advantage that we should reap from a legal protection of complete copyright in authors. We should have the works of British and other European writers in a better form than that in which they are now, almost of necessity, presented to us. The "American" book-buyer, as well as the author, would profit by the act of justice ; for the original publisher, having such an immense market thrown open to him, would publish for a large instead of a small sale, and would in the style of his issues and the proportion of his profit consult the tastes and the pockets of his new customers. The British public would also profit by the change ; for it would necessarily cheapen the price of books in the British market. The " American" purchaser of a British author's book would then have, at a trifling advance over that which he now pays, a book which he could read with comfort and keep with pleasure, instead of the flimsy, eye-destroying thing which he now throws away worn and shattered by once passing through the hands of his family.

The author's right is to a remuneration from all who use his labors, and not merely that which is called by some a " fair reward " for those labors. They are worth just what they will bring him from those who use them.

> " For what's the worth of anything,
> But so much money as 'twill bring ?"

Who made you, or me, or our Representatives in Congress assembled, the judge of what is a fair reward for any man's work? Do we say to the merchant, or to the ship-carpenter, or to the farmer, You shall have a fair reward for your labors, but no more? It is idle, it is worse, it is mean, to attempt to stigmatize copyright by calling it a " tax upon knowledge." It would ~~invole~~ a tax just as any determination to pay an honest debt involves a tax—no more.

It is attempted to conceal the glaring injustice of the appropriation of the author's right to the fruits of his labor by the plea that the " public good " demands this confiscation by society of the property of individuals—that the productions of authors are so necessary to the " welfare of society" that it must take forcible and unrepaying possession of them in whole or in part. The scurviest politician that ever got him glass eyes, and seemed to see the thing he saw not, never used an argument more degrading to himself and those whom he addressed. It is a bad doctrine ; and it is the worse because there is in it some semblance of truth. The public *is* in a measure the gainer by the denial or the restriction of the rights of authors ; but in like manner would it be profited by the appropriation, in whole or in part, of the labors of other men who are producers. Only the direst emergency can justify the absorption of individual possession by society. It is right to blow up a man's house without his consent if so doing will save a whole city from the flames, or to burn it to protect a community from deadly infection ; but it is not right to do even this without full compensation ; and the right to commit such violence is jealously regarded as the most exceptional right possessed by society. Teach people that the good of a thousand men will justify the systematic robbery of one, and the foundation of individual property crumbles, the distinction between honesty and dishonesty is obliterated. If a thousand may despoil one, why not five hundred ? if five hundred, why not fifty ? if fifty, why not five ? The doctrine would suit well a nation of footpads. Justice is more beneficent than cheap reading. Honesty is better than culture.

One objection to the claim of the foreign author for copyright in this country has been made, and has been urged so strongly and with such seeming good faith, that it may well be considered for a moment seriously, notwithstanding its absurdity. It is that the people of foreign countries, if injured in life or limb or goods, have no claim on the Government of the United States to protect them or to give them redress ; why, then it is asked, should foreign authors make such a claim ? why should they be made exceptions to this rule ? It should not be necessary to say that the citizens of foreign countries *have* a claim for protection and redress against wrongs done to them or to their property in the United States. But a European author has none ; nor can he have any such claim until some way is found and adopted of allowing him and the citizens of the United States to make a free bargain with him as to their use of his labor. This consideration has thus far been entirely disregarded, and will probably be disregarded for a long time hereafter. The rights of no man, the rights of no community to do what they will with their own, and to buy and sell where they please and of whom they please, have been allowed a feather's weight in the previous discussions of the question. This whole subject is simply a matter of the interest of publishers and manufacturers, in which the rights of authors are no more considered than those of the horses who draw the manufacturers' drays. Publishers who treat native authors more than fairly (and I, for one, own to having been treated with the most generous consideration by all the publishers, two excepted, with whom I have had dealings) are relentless about this matter of giving British authors control of their works in this country. And they have the whole legislative power with them. Mr. Arnold and all his countrymen who are interested in the subject may rest assured that, whatever the talk may be, now or hereafter, there is not the slightest intention of making any radical change in this matter. And yet he and they may possibly discover, from what has gone before, that at least a very considerable number of that American community which, as he supposes, has "the spirit of a middle class society" of his own race, and who, as he says (and he must know) "have not shown a spirit of delicacy in dealing with authors, even with their own," but who deal with them "as much as Manchester, perhaps, might be disposed, if left to itself, to deal with them" (a point as to which he certainly is authority, except "perhaps" in Manchester), are moved in this mat-

ter by an impulse higher than mere delicacy—an
impulse which perhaps he might call something
within them, not themselves, that makes for righteousness.

There is talk now of a treaty between Great
Britain and the United States to secure reciprocal
protection in both countries for the writers of
both ; and it is said that the draft of such a treaty
has been sent from the State Department of the
United States to our minister at the court of St.
James's. But even if the proposal should be accepted, and the treaty made, there seems to be
good reason for believing that neither the rights of
British authors nor the interests of their "American" publishers would be secure. For copyright
is not properly the subject of a treaty. This matter has been placed by the Constitution in the
hands of Congress ; and it is settled law that a
power granted by the Constitution to Congress is
exclusive. The House of Representatives might
pass a law conformed to such a treaty ; but if they
did so, with the consent of the Senate and the approval of the President (the treaty-making pow-
ers), what use of the treaty ? and at any time such
a law might be repealed by Congress. There is,
however, no probability that such a law would be
passed ; and the treaty would be set at naught, and
successfully, by " piratical " publishers, British
and " American." And according to the Constitution (Art. I., Sec. viii., 8), Congress has the
power of securing authors and inventors an exclusive right in their writings and inventions only
" for limited times." If Congress, then, were

willing to provide by law for the security of authors in all their rights, it could not do so without an amendment of the Constitution. The maimed rights and the crippled control over their own works which they now possess are theirs, not by reason of a recognition of their natural rights, but as a boon conferred upon them to promote the progress of science and the useful arts. And if copyright laws must be accepted as conferring a right instead of restricting it, with what reason can a Legislature be asked to recognize in aliens a right which is for citizens themselves the mere creation of a statute ? *

An international copyright law which prescribes when, where, how, and by whom the foreign author shall publish his book, is somewhat insulting, and is against the interests of most foreign authors, and of all foreign publishers ; which, I think, has been made clear in the foregoing pages.

There are, indeed, but three conceivable courses in regard to this question :

First, to recognize the author's right of property in his work simply and absolutely.

Second (the Philadelphia way), to deny it simply and absolutely, and to take, " convey," or " nym" his work for the pleasure of the public and the profit of publishers.

---

* This view of the constitutional aspect of the question was set forth by me in a brief postscript to the " American View of the Copyright Question," in May, 1868. It was afterwards repeated, almost in the same words, by a writer signing himself " Justice," who discussed the question, adversely, in three long communications to the N. Y. *Times,* in March and April, 1872.

Third (that proposed by the " Appleton Bill"), to admit the right, but to say that in order that certain book manufacturers may make money, and certain people get their reading very cheap, you will set the author's rights at naught and give him what you please, on condition that he allows you and no one else to sell or to print his book in " America."

In conclusion, I commend to the reader's attention the two articles of the appendix to this discussion : the first, from the Rev. Dr. Prime, President of the Executive Committee of the Copyright Association, and editor of the New York *Observer*, which presents the whole question in a nutshell ; the second, a business view of the subject taken from Mr. George Haven Putnam's address, delivered in New York, January 29, 1879—the most thoughtful and practical utterance upon this question which has been heard from the publishers' benches. Yet even in reading these it should be remembered that this question is properly one not of the interests of publishers, but of the rights of authors ; that publishers, as a body, have no interest in literature except as merchandise ; and that no publisher can have a rightful interest in any book unless it is given to him by the author.

APPENDIX.

[*From Putnam's Magazine for May.*]

THE RIGHT OF COPYRIGHT.

A Concise Statement of the Question.

BY S. IRENÆUS PRIME.

I.

Proudhon's motto was, " Property is robbery." He denied the *right* of *property.* All things, in his view, belong to all men in common. The earth, the air, fire, water, the natural forces, all sources of wealth, are common stock, and the results of their use are the universal heritage of mankind.

II.

H. C. Carey has promulgated a theory of copyright substantially on the same basis. Ideas are the common property of mankind. Facts are everybody's facts. Words are free to all men. He says : " Examine Macaulay's ' History of England,' and you will find that the body is composed of what is common property." He says the same of Prescott, Bancroft, and Webster : " They did nothing but reproduce ideas that were common property." Of Scott and Irving he says, they " made no contribution to knowledge."

III.

Therefore, the author of a book has no right of property in the book he has made. He took the common stock and worked it over ; and one man has just as good a right to it as another. A law to give an author the exclusive control of his book is not founded in justice. The public are deprived of their rights if the author is allowed to be the *owner* of his own works. Property in books is robbery.

IV.

There is no substantial difference between the Proudhon theory of *no property* and the Carey theory of *no property in books*. The first breaks down all business ; the second destroys all business in books. If Smith shall have the same right with Jones to the house Jones builds, Jones will not be apt to build houses. If Carey has the same right to Motley's " History" that Motley has, Motley will not be inclined to write histories for Carey.

A disciple of Carey has recently put forth a pamphlet in which he takes the position that " the word *property* is only applicable to material substances ;" and " a person's ideas or thoughts are his intellectual property only so long as they remain unuttered and unknown to others." It is a reproach upon our country, and upon the Christianity of the age, that a doctrine like this is avowed by any civilized man among us. Noah Webster defines the word thus :

Property.—The exclusive right of possessing, enjoying, and disposing of a thing ; ownership. Prior occupancy of land and of wild animals, gives to the possessor the property of them. The labor of inventing, making, or producing any thing, constitutes one of the highest and most indefeasible titles to property.

And that no possible misunderstanding may arise as to the meaning, he defines again :

Literary Property.—No right or title to a thing can be so perfect as that which is created by a man's own labor and invention. The exclusive right of a man to his literary productions, and to the use of them for his own profit, is entire and perfect, as the faculties employed, and labor bestowed, are entirely and perfectly his own. On what principle, then, can a legislature or a court determine that an author can enjoy only a *temporary property* in his own productions? If a man's right to his own *productions in writing* is as perfect as to the *productions* of his farm, or his shop, how can the former be abridged or limited, while the latter is held without limitations ! Why do the productions of manual labor reach higher in the scale of rights or property than the productions of the intellect ?

V.

Civilized society has recognized the right of property in all ages and lands, even independently of the eighth and tenth commandments. The right of an author to the fruit of his labor and intellect is as perfect and indefeasible as the right of a farmer to his crop. Common materials are employed by men in all pursuits, but whatever each man's industry, genius, or skill produces, is *his own*, his property ; and he who takes it from him without his consent, or uses it against his will, is a thief and a robber. This is the essence of property in an invention, or a photograph, or a map, or a book.

VI.

Therefore, law shields an author by a *copyright*, and all persons are restrained from publishing his works without his consent. The historian composes his history, and has an exclusive *right* to it. The poet owns his own poem. The dramatist owns the drama that he writes. The author has law to shield him against robbery, as the merchant or farmer has. This right is not a concession by society to the author, as Mr. Carey says it is. The right is absolute and intrinsic as any other right recognized among men.

VII.

Limiting the time during which this right of the author shall continue to be recognized by law is an error arising from the confusion of ideas as to the nature of the right. The right being perfect, and all rights and duties being reciprocal, it is the duty of Government to make the protection coextensive with the right which is perpetual. When it is made legal for a man to live rent-free in a house after he has paid rent for it twenty-eight years, or to have a newspaper for nothing when he has been a paying subscriber forty years, then, but not till then, should authors be deprived of their property, after the public has paid for the use of it a limited number of years.

VIII.

American authors have a just claim upon their Government for such legislation as will enable them to enjoy the benefit of their works when they are wanted in foreign countries. Such protection requires reciprocity ; and if it be just to American authors to secure their rights in foreign lands, it is right and necessary that foreign authors have corresponding protection in the United States.

IX.

An International Copyright Law is, therefore, simple justice between man and man. The author's *moral* right being perfect, as the right of any other person to his property, Government is bound to make the *legal* right commensurate therewith. Unless we make war upon all property, and abolish the distinctions of *meum* and *tuum* altogether, we must admit the duty of governments to secure the rights of authors in their property at home and abroad. And as law protects the American merchant's gold in London, so should law, by reciprocal legislation, make the author's right to his property equally secure.

X.

The slave-trade, once regarded as moral and respectable traffic, was prosecuted by the best men in the Church and world.

Lotteries were once legal and reputable, and the Government, churches, schools, and individuals participated in their profits without scruple.

Now the slave-trade is justly punished as piracy, and lotteries as gambling and robbery. But the slave-trade and lotteries are now no more in reality offensive to good morals than they were when both flourished under the wing of the Church and the State. The public conscience having been enlightened and quickened, it is now a subject for wonder that honest and honorable men were ever engaged in either. It is hardly credible, but it is true, that the good people of Newport, Rhode Island, had twelve ships trading at one time with Cuba and Surinam, '' bringing molasses to be distilled into New England rum, which was sent to Africa in exchange for negro slaves.''

When the public conscience is awakened to the right of authors in their works, the Carey theory will be looked upon by all conscientious persons as flagitious and immoral as Proudhon's doctrine or the Newport trade in rum and negroes.

Then Government will not suffer its people to plunder a foreign author nor allow its own authors to be plundered in foreign lands ; and then no honest publisher will violate the rights of an author, whether the law shields him or not.

XI.

It is always for the interest of individuals and communities, in the long run, to do right ; it never is for their interest to do wrong. In this case the interests of the publisher, the printer, the paper-maker, and the reader, are promoted by doing justly by the author. The partial protection of an author's rights which the law now gives is a powerful stimulant to literary labor. Literature cannot be a profession without it. Men will not plant orchards if the fruit is free to all comers. Men will not devote their lives to making books unless they can live by it. The Copyright Law gives them this security. And an international copyright law would add a market, in many millions of people, to that now enjoyed by American authors. This encouragement would enhance the production in proportion to the new demand. The amount of British literature offered to our market would be vastly increased ; and American authorship, protected throughout the realms of the English language, would hasten to win the same triumphs that American genius has achieved in the mechanical arts. The healthful competition in the manufacture of books thus stimulated would keep down the prices to the lowest remunerative point,* and the ex-

* One of the most specious and effective arguments reiterated against international justice in this matter, is the statement that, if British authors are paid for the use of their books in this country, an enormous addition will be made to the price of the books—that we shall have to pay the prices of new books in England—a guinea and a half for a novel, etc., etc.

The fallacy, not to say dishonesty, of this statement, may be readily shown by any intelligent and candid publisher.

The copyright of an English book being vested in an American citizen, and the book being manufactured in this country (as Mr. Baldwin's bill proposes), it will be for the *selfish* interest of the publisher to adapt the book to the tastes and means of the largest

tended field would furnish a demand for books so vast as to require all the energies of our book-trade to supply.

In this case, as always, " Honesty is the best policy." And degrading as it is to appeal to such a sentiment where the right is so palpable, we may rejoice in the fact that the *interests* of publishers and readers are here identical with the rights of authors.

number of purchasers—in just the same way as he would manage a book by an American author.

When it is evident that the sale of five thousand, ten thousand, or fifty thousand copies at a dollar will "*pay*" better than five hundred copies at five dollars, the publisher's *policy* is self-evident. His interests are identified, both with those of the author and with those of the great mass of readers. To illustrate this obvious truth, it is sufficient to mention the last new and notable copyright book—Beecher's "Norwood." It was competent for Mr. Bonner, owner of the copyright, or the monopoly, and Mr. Scribner, the publisher, to determine that the price of the book shall be three or five dollars, and nobody could say nay. What do they do? They voluntarily and wisely sell it for a dollar and a half—a *less* price actually than is now asked for most reprinted books of the same size which pay *no* copyright ; and yet the author in this case is not merely justly, but very liberally compensated. The publisher makes the book at a moderate price, because he makes more money by doing so.

Again, it is the publisher's obvious policy now, and it would continue to be, under an international law, to adapt his books to the market. If there is a call for fine editions as well as cheap ones, he will make those also. Another copyright-book may be mentioned—Irving's " Sketch-Book." The publisher finds it expedient to make an edition of this at twenty dollars per copy ; but he offers the buyer, at the same moment, other editions of the same book, at ten dollars, at two dollars, and at seventy-five cents. Each of these, observe, is a copyright-book, and the author's part is the same. These specimens illustrate a general principle.

Suppose an international law should cause a slight increase of price in order that the author may be compensated ; will the reader grudge this ?

But the payment by the publisher of five or ten per cent, or of a fixed sum, for the copyright of a book, whether by an American or a British author, under the proposed law, *does not* necessarily increase the price of the book. It is not so much a tax on the purchaser as it is a premium paid by the publisher for greater security to property in which he invests money for himself and his children.

This security, as Mr. Baldwin shows in his report, will inure to the benefit rather than the injury of all classes of readers, as well as of author and publisher.—EDITOR.

EXTRACT FROM MR. GEORGE HAVEN PUT-NAM'S ADDRESS ON INTERNATIONAL COPYRIGHT.

[Delivered in New York, January 29, 1879.]

REJECTING the Elderkin-Sherman suggestion of an open market for republishing, as in no way effecting the objects desired ; the Baldwin-Cox plan of giving protection only to books of which the type had been set and the printing done in this country, as narrow in principle and uneconomic in practice ; and the Bristed-Morgan proposition to extend the right of copyright without limitation or restriction, as not giving sufficient consideration to the business requirements, and as at present impracticable to carry into effect—we would recommend a measure based upon the suggestion of the British Commission, coupled with one or two of the provisions that have been included in the several American schemes :

" 1. That the title of the foreign work be registered in the United States simultaneously with its publication abroad.

" 2. That the work be republished in the United States within six months of its publication abroad.

"3. That for a limited term—say, ten years—the stipulation should be made that the republishing be done by an American citizen.

" 4. That for the same term of years the copyright protection be given to those books only that have been printed and bound in this country, the privilege being accorded of importing foreign stereotypes and electrotypes of cuts.

" 5. That, subject to these provisions, the foreign author or his assigns shall be accorded the same privileges now conceded to an American author."

I believe that in the course of time the general laws of trade would and ought to so regulate the arrangements for supplying the American public with books that, if there were no restriction as to the nationality of the publisher, or as to the importation of printed volumes, the author would select the publishing agent, English or American, who could serve him to best advantage, and that that agent would be found to be the man who would prepare for the largest possible circle of American readers the editions best suited to their wants.

The foreign author would before long recognize that it was to his interest to be represented by the publisher who understood the market most thoroughly, and who had the best facilities for supplying it. If English publishers settling here could excel our American houses in this understanding and in these facilities, they ought to be at liberty to do so, and it would be for the interest of the public that no hindrances should be placed in their way.

*   *   *   *   *   *   *

I can, however, imagine no state of affairs in which it would be economical or desirable to insist upon two settings of type for a book designed for different groups of English-speaking readers ; and the more generally this first and most important part of the cost of a book can be economized by being divided between the two markets, the greater the advantage in the end to author, public, and publisher.

THE END

MEMORANDUM.

WHILE these few pages have been awaiting, in the rush and turmoil of preparation for the Christmas holidays, their turn to be bound up and put forth, yet another "movement" in regard to copyright has been set vigorously on foot. It is just what might have been looked for under the circumstances. The project of a treaty is scouted by the originators of the new plan, who would have a law which, briefly, would give copyright to an alien author on these conditions only: that his book should be wholly manufactured in the United States; that it should be published here by a citizen of the United States; that a contract for its publication should be made within *two months* of its publication in Europe (all right of the author here being otherwise lost); and finally, that a list of all books so contracted for should be furnished to the Customs officers, and that all copies of them coming from abroad should be confiscated. The openly avowed purpose of the proposed law is to disable the alien author from preventing or postponing, at any time, for any period, or for any reason, the publication of his book in the United States, and to exclude absolutely all copies of the edition authorized by him, even if people in the United States wish to obtain them, and to pay him and his publisher for them. For example, Mr. Justin McCarthy's *History of Our Own Times* has been largely imported here, and is so much sought after in the original edition, although the price of it is $18, that copies are now with difficulty procured. This book has been reprinted complete in a large pamphlet form, and is sold for 40 cents. The effect of the proposed law would be that if an "American" publisher chose to issue a book of this sort in such a form, or in any other, people in the United States would be prohibited from supplying themselves with copies of the London edition. The prohibition would be absolute and effective, for it would be put in force by the Customs officers, according to their lists. A better example of tyranny, pure and simple, than this proposed scheme of international justice—the victims being both authors and the public—it would be hard to find in modern history.

December 23d, 1880.